THE SESAME STREET 1,2,3 STORYBOOK

WRITTEN BY
Emily Perl Kingsley   Jeffrey Moss
Norman Stiles   Daniel Wilcox

PICTURES BY
Joseph Mathieu   Kelly Oechsli
Mel Crawford   Bob Taylor

and featuring Jim Henson's Muppets

RANDOM HOUSE · CHILDREN'S TELEVISION WORKSHOP

CONTENTS

Quality Printing by:
National Litho
4206 Shannon Drive
Baltimore, MD 21213 U.S.A.

Library of Congress Cataloging in Publication Data: Main entry under title: The Sesame Street 1, 2, 3 storybook. SUMMARY: The Sesame Street muppet puppets star in ten humorous stories, each about a number from one to ten. [1. Humorous stories. 2. Counting books] I. Kingsley. Emily Perl. II. Random House. New York. III. Children's Television Workshop. PZ7.S4895 [E] 73-2768. ISBN 0-394-82694-9   ISBN 0-394-92694-3 (lib. bdg.)

1

Bert's Bath

"Hey, Bert," said Ernie one bright sunny day. "Let's go out and play some football."

"Ernie, I can't go play football," said Bert. "Can't you see I'm going to take a bath now? I can't play football."

"Gee, Bert," said Ernie, "you don't have everything you need to take a bath. You need **1** more thing."

"Oh?" said Bert. "I do?"

7

"Yes!" said Ernie. "You need **1 rubber duckie** to keep you company. Here it is."

"O.K., Ernie," Bert said. "Thanks a lot. Now I'm going to take my bath."

"Wait a second, Bert," Ernie said. "I forgot. You'll need **1** more thing in your bath. You might get hungry, so here is **1 sandwich** for you to eat."

"A sandwich?" cried Bert. "How can I eat a sandwich in the bathtub?"

"You're right," said Ernie. "You'll need **1** more thing. You don't want to get crumbs in the tubby...so you will need **1 table** to eat your sandwich on."

8

"Come on, Ernie," groaned Bert. "I can't take a bath with all that stuff."

"Of course you can't!" said Ernie. "You need **1** more thing. You need to have some nice music to listen to. You need **1 piano**."

"Ernie!" yelled Bert. "This is ridiculous. I can't play the piano while I take a bath!"

"You certainly can't," Ernie said. "How silly of me. Just **1** more thing and then everything will be ready."

"There you are," said Ernie. "**1 elephant** to play the piano for you."

"Ernie!" shouted Bert. "Will you look at this! With your **just 1 more thing,** and **1 more thing,** you've filled up the whole bathub and there's no room for me in there! Now I can't take a bath at all!"

"In that case," said Ernie, "how about going out to play a little football with me, huh, Bert?"

Sherlock Hemlock
in
"The Mysterious Stranger"

14

The Monster's Three Wishes

Once there lived a little monster
In a kingdom far away.
And a very strange thing happened
As he brushed his teeth one day.

As he squeezed his tube of toothpaste,
Deepest thunder shook the skies.
And suddenly a genie stood
Before his very eyes.

"I'm the genie of the toothpaste,"
Said the genie with a laugh.
"I've been trapped inside
　　　　　that toothpaste tube
For 3 weeks and a half.
You squeezed the tube and set me free
So here is what I'll do—
I'll let you have 3 wishes
And I'll make them all come true."

"Oh boy!" exclaimed the monster,
"Wow! 3 wishes just for me!
Now let me think and then decide
What my first wish will be."

Now my favorite thing is cookies,
Thought the monster with a grin.
*But first I'll wish for something nice
To keep my cookies in.
I would like a million cookies,
But before I use that wish...*

"Hey, Genie," said the monster,
"Will you please bring me a <u>dish</u>?"

"Will I ever!" said the genie,
"For your wish is my command."
And instantly a dish appeared
Right in the monster's hand.

"Hey, I did it!" cried the genie.
"Wow! I haven't lost my touch!"
"It's a nice dish," said the monster,
"But it won't hold very much."

The monster thought of all the cookies
That he'd soon get with his wish.
And he knew a million cookies
Couldn't fit on one small dish.

He would need something much bigger.
So the monster said, "Hey, Genie!
I would like a great big box...
This plate is much too teeny!"

"You want a box? You've got it,"
Said the genie with a smirk.
And instantly a box appeared.
The monster cried, "Nice work!"

But although the box was pretty big
And could hold lots of stuff—
Could it hold a million cookies...?
It just wasn't big enough.

So the monster called the genie
And said, "Boy, am I in luck!
Since you'll give me what I wish for...
How about a great big <u>truck</u>?"

And right away a truck appeared
Before the monster's eyes.
"Fantastic!" cried the monster.
"It is just the perfect size!"

"It will hold a million cookies,
And I'll never have to worry.
And that is what I wish for!
Give me cookies now! Please hurry!"

"I am sorry," said the genie,
"For though cookies are delicious,
I *cannot* give them to you
'Cause you've used up your **3** wishes."

"Oh, no!" exclaimed the monster.
"Is it true? I just can't tell.
For although I'm good at eating things,
I do not count so well."

"Let us count these things together,"
Said the genie, "and you'll see—
The <u>dish</u> is **1,** the <u>box</u> is **2,**
And then the <u>truck</u> makes **3.**"
"**3** things! You're right," the monster said,
"Now what am I to do?
I've used up my **3** wishes
And I'm very hungry, too!"

"Gee, that's too bad," the genie said,
"But now my job's complete."
"I'm so *hungry*," said the monster,
"Oh, I need something to *eat!*"

"I'm sad your wish for cookies
Can't come true," the genie said.
"That's okay," replied the monster........

"...I'll just eat the <u>truck</u> instead!"

And as the monster ate the truck,
The genie disappeared,
Saying, "I have seen a lot of things—
But boy...is *that* guy weird!"

4

Oscar and the Number Four

y name is Oscar the Grouch and my favorite number is the number 4. Let me tell you 4 reasons why.

First of all, I like the number 4 because there are 4 wheels on a garbage truck. Count them. And I love garbage trucks because of all the wonderful yucchy trash inside!

SANITATION

I also like the number **4** because a skunk has **4** legs.
Count them. A skunk makes a terrible smell that makes
everybody run away. Heh-heh.

A table has **4** legs, too. And a
table is a perfect thing to sit at
when I eat my strawberry ice
cream sundae with pickles
and sardines on top!

And last of all, I like the number **4** because the page of a book has **4** corners. Count them. And after you count the corners, turn that page and then I won't have to look at you any more!! *Good-by!*

26

Sam Shows Big Bird Five

29

Six Monsters in the Restaurant

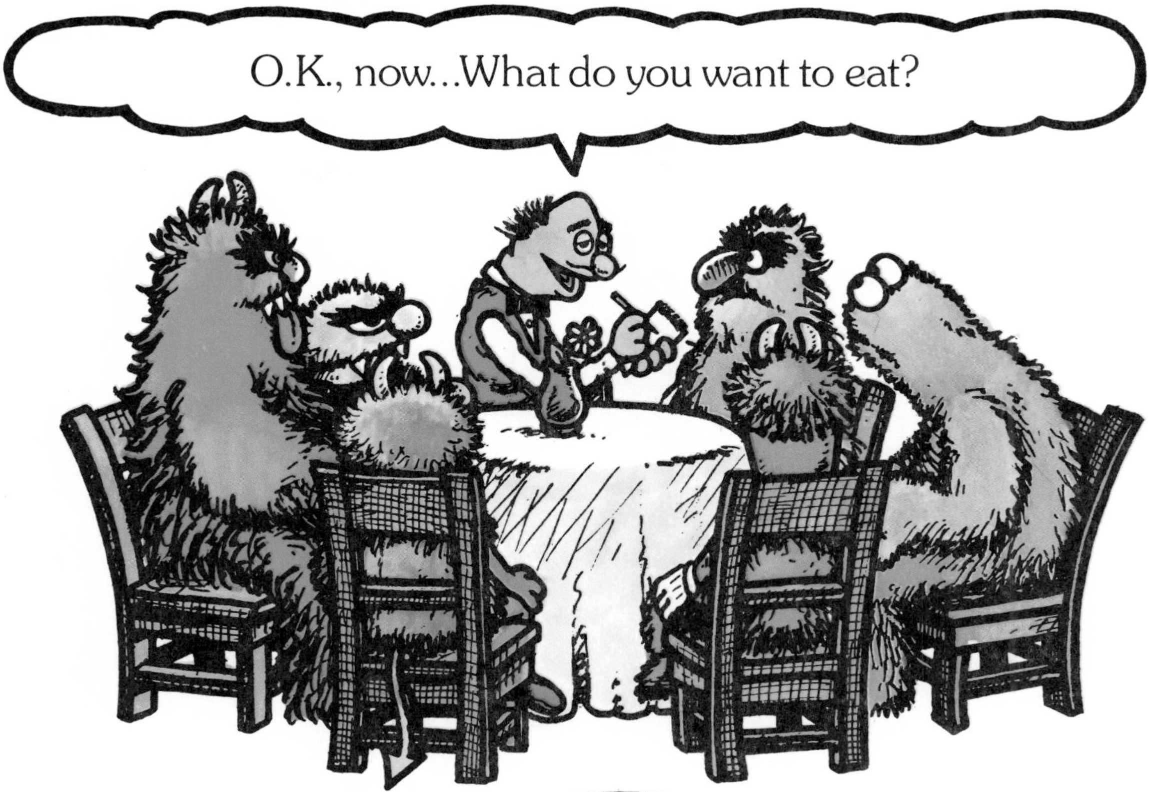
O.K., now...What do you want to eat?

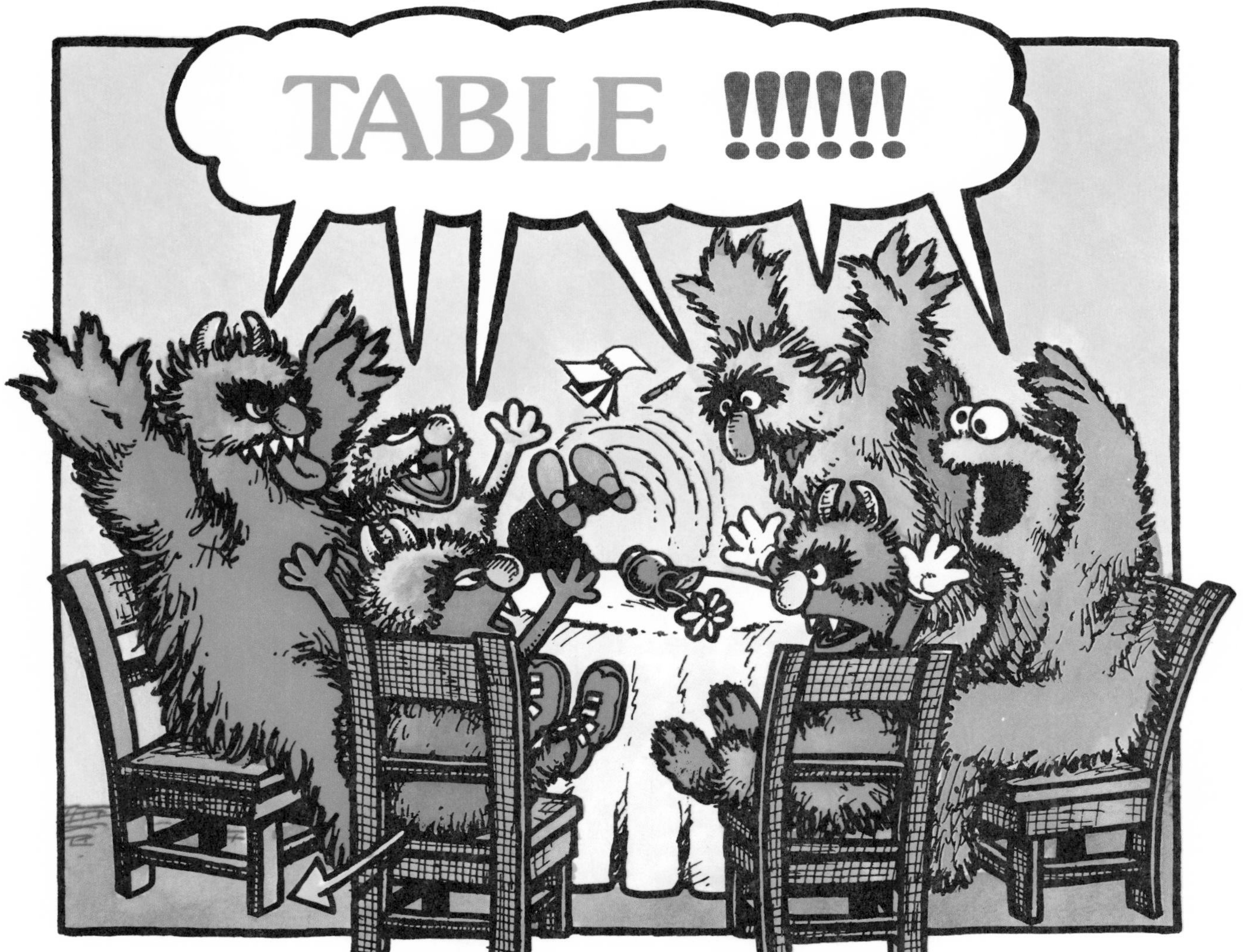
TABLE !!!!!!

36

Goldie-Snuffle and the Seven Bears

One day a beautiful, golden-haired Snuffle-upagus named Goldie-Snuffle was walking through the woods with her friend Big Bird.

"Goldie," said Big Bird, "you have never met *any* of my friends, and they all say there is no such thing as a Snuffle-upagus. Will you come meet my friends, **the 7 Bears**? They live right around the corner."

"Oh, goody!" said Goldie-Snuffle.

Big Bird and Goldie-Snuffle came to the
cottage of the **7** Bears. They knocked
on the door, but nobody answered. "There's
nobody home, Goldie," said Big Bird.

"Oh, dear," said Goldie-
Snuffle. "Well let's go in
anyway." And in they went.

Inside the cottage were **7** chairs. "I think
I'll sit down," said Goldie-Snuffle.

Big Bird said, "But, Goldie, some of these
chairs are small, some are big, and some are
in-between. How do you know which chair is
just right for you?"

"I'll sit in them all," said
Goldie-Snuffle.

So she sat in all of the
chairs, one at a time. And
she broke all of the chairs...
one at a time.

"They were *all* too small
for you, Goldie," said
Big Bird.

Next, Goldie-Snuffle found a
table with **7** bowls of spaghetti
on it.

Goldie-Snuffle said, "Some of
these bowls of spaghetti
are too hot, and some of them are
too cold, and some are just
right. But I really love
spaghetti, so I think
I'll eat them all."

And she did.

When she finished eating, Goldie-Snuffle said, "I think I'll lie down."

In the cottage were **7** beds.

Big Bird said, "Goldie, some of these beds are small, some are big, and some are in-between. But they're all too small for you."

"Then I'll lie down on them all at once," said Goldie-Snuffle.

And she did. And she broke them all at once.

"Oh, dear," said Goldie-Snuffle, "I have to go. So long, Bird."

"But Goldie," said Big Bird, "the cottage is a mess, and the 7 Bears are just getting home. Stay and help clean up."

"I'd like to, Bird, but it's time for my nap," said Goldie-Snuffle. And she left.

When the **7** Bears saw their house, they said, "My goodness! Somebody broke all our chairs…"

"…and ate all our spaghetti…"

"…and crushed all our beds. Big Bird, what happened?"

43

"Oh, I can explain," said Big Bird. "Goldie-Snuffle was here. She's a beautiful, golden-haired Snuffle-upagus, and she loves spaghetti, and she's very big, and…"

"*Snuffle-upagus?*" said the **7** Bears. "There's no such thing as a Snuffle-upagus. Big Bird, you sure have some imagination!"

King Hungry the Eighth

King Hungry the Eighth
ordered dinner one day.
He called for his cooks
to appear right away.
"I'm hungry," he said,
"so bring me my plate,
and make sure the things on it
all number **8**!"

They brought him **8** hot dogs and **8** toasted rolls,
8 pickles, **8** pretzels, **8** donuts with holes.

The King ate them all and he wiped off his chin,
and smiled and said, "Not a bad way to begin."

"Now bring me," the King said, "**8** French fried potatoes.
And **8** lemon pies with **8** juicy tomatoes."

He swallowed it all with **8** pieces of bread.
"I'm not called King Hungry for nothing!" he said.

So they brought him **8** pizzas
with sausage and cheese,
and the King gulped them down
just as quick as you please.

Then he gobbled **8** turkeys
with stuffing and yams,
and **8** black-eyed peas,
and then **8** boiled hams.

Said the King to the cooks, "My, but eating is fun!"
Now bring me dessert so my meal will be done!"

For dessert the King polished off
8 chocolate cakes…

And went off to bed
with **8** *big tummy-aches!!*

The Story of the Nine Dragons

Once upon a time, in the faraway kingdom of St. George, there lived a baseball team. There were **9** players on the team.

One day, as they reached their practice field, **9** dragons leaped out of the woods, breathing fire and smoke and yelling, *"Arkle-Snarkle Higgeldy Snoo!"*

This frightened the baseball players and they ran away. After all, you'd be frightened, too, if **9** dragons leaped out of the woods while you were playing baseball.

Every day when the **9** baseball players got to the ball field the same thing would happen.

After this had gone on for several weeks, one of the players decided it was time to do something about the dragons.

"I've got an idea how to get rid of those dragons," he said. And he told his idea to the other players.

So the next day, each of the **9** players got a big feather and went out to the baseball field.

When the **9** dragons jumped out of the forest, the **9** players took the **9** feathers and tickled the **9** dragons on their tummies. The dragons rolled over on their backs and giggled dragon-giggles and kicked their feet in the air.

But when they were finished being tickled, the dragons jumped up and breathed fire and smoke and yelled, *"Arkel-Snarkle Higgeldy Snoo,"* and frightened the players away again.

So the **9** baseball players decided that tickling the dragons wasn't such a good idea after all.

Suddenly, the team's right fielder (who also happened to be a dragon expert) stepped forward.

"I just happen to be a dragon expert," she said, "and I have an idea. Here's my dragon book. Why don't we look in it and see what *Arkle-Snarkle Higgeldy Snoo* means?"

"It's so crazy it just might work," said the third baseman.

The next day, when the **9** baseball players went out to the field, they pulled behind them a great big wagon with a cover over it.

Once again the **9** dragons jumped out of the woods, breathed fire and smoke, and yelled, *"Arkle-Snarkle Higgeldy Snoo! Arkle-Snarkle Higgeldy Snoo!!"*

The players quickly pulled the cover off the wagon and, lo and behold, there were **9** great big dragon-sized baseball caps, **9** great big dragon-sized baseball mitts, and **9** great big dragon-sized baseball bats!

For the right fielder's dragon book had told them that *"Arkle-Snarkle Higgeldy Snoo"* is dragon-talk for, "We want to play baseball, too!"

So every day the **9** baseball players went out to the baseball field and met the **9** dragons on the dragon team...and they played baseball.

So if you happen to be walking through the woods one day and **9** dragons jump out at you, breathing fire and smoke and yelling, *"Arkle-Snarkle Higgeldy Snoo,"* don't be afraid. Chances are they just want to play baseball!

59

Grover Buys Ten Balloons

63